❦ PROFILES OF GREAT ❦
BLACK AMERICANS

Male Writers

❦❦

Edited by Richard Rennert
Introduction by Coretta Scott King

||| A Chelsea House
||| Multibiography

Chelsea House Publishers
New York · Philadelphia

Copyright © 1994 by Chelsea House Publishers, a division of
Main Line Book Co. All rights reserved. Printed and bound in the
United States of America.

First Printing

1 3 5 7 9 8 6 4 2

Library of Congress Cataloging-in-Publication Data

Male writers / edited by Richard Rennert; introduction by
Coretta Scott King.
    p. cm.—(Profiles of great black Americans) (A Chelsea House
multibiography)
    Includes bibliographical references and index.
Contents: James Baldwin—Charles Chesnutt—Paul Laurence
Dunbar—Ralph Ellison—Alex Haley—Chester Himes—
Langston Hughes—Richard Wright.
    ISBN   0-7910-2061-4.
                0-7910-2062-2 (pbk.)
1. Afro-American authors—Biography—Juvenile literature
2. Afro-American men—Biography—Juvenile literature.
3. Men authors—Biography—Juvenile literature. [1. Authors,
American. 2. Afro-Americans—Biography.] I. Rennert, Richard
Scott, 1956– . II. Series. III. Series: A Chelsea House
multibiography
PS153.N5M25 1994   93-11412
810.9'896073—dc20   CIP
    [B]   AC

❧ CONTENTS ❧

❦ INTRODUCTION ❦
by Coretta Scott King

This book is about black Americans who served society through the excellence of their achievements. It forms a part of the rich history of black men and women in America—a history of stunning accomplishments in every field of human endeavor, from literature and art to science, industry, education, diplomacy, athletics, jurisprudence, even polar exploration.

Not all of the people in this history had the same ideals, but I think you will find something that all of them had in common. Like Martin Luther King, Jr., they all decided to become "drum majors" and serve humanity. In that principle—whether it was expressed in books, inventions, or song—they found something outside themselves to use as a goal and a guide. Something that showed them a way to serve others instead of only living for themselves.

Reading the stories of these courageous men and women not only helps us discover the principles that we will use to guide our own lives but also teaches us about our black heritage and about America itself. It is crucial for us to know the heroes and heroines of our history and to realize that the price we paid in our struggle for equality in America was dear. But we must also understand that we have gotten as far as we have partly because America's democratic system and ideals made it possible.

We are still struggling with racism and prejudice. But the great men and women in this series are a tribute to the spirit of our democratic ideals and the system in which they have flourished. And that makes their stories special and worth knowing.

JAMES BALDWIN

Novelist, essayist, and passionate critic of American race relations, James Arthur Baldwin was born on August 2, 1924, in the black community of Harlem in New York City. He was the oldest in a family of nine brothers and sisters, and his childhood was one of poverty and hardship. His stepfather, a part-time preacher who worked in a local bottling plant, nurtured a fierce hatred of white people and was a stern disciplinarian whom the young James could never please. His mother worked as a maid. A small, frail-looking boy with wide eyes and a broad grin whose classmates at Frederick Douglass Junior High School would often bully, James took refuge from the bleakness and cruelty of his environment by immersing himself in reading and writing. He discovered the New York Public Library in midtown Manhattan and went there frequently, and he began to write stories and essays on Harlem life for his school paper.

At the age of 14, Baldwin experienced a religious conversion and began to preach at the Fireside Pentecostal Assembly, one of Harlem's many storefront churches. At the same time, he also began to attend De Witt Clinton High School in the Bronx, where he befriended a group of white students who shared his growing interest in literature and avant-garde ideas. By the time he graduated from high school in 1942, he had abandoned his preaching and determined to become a writer.

In the summer of 1943, with Harlem shaken by riots as a result of the shooting of a black man by white police officers, Baldwin, as he wrote in his famous essay "Notes of a Native Son," decided that he would have to leave the community or be consumed by the poverty, desperation, and rage he saw all around him. He moved into a small apartment in Greenwich Village in lower Manhattan. During the day he worked as a waiter, busboy, and dishwasher in local restaurants, and at night he continued to write.

In 1945, Baldwin met the novelist Richard Wright, whose *Native Son* was the most critically acclaimed and commercially successful novel ever written by a black American. Wright offered the aspiring writer much encouragement, and Baldwin began to write book reviews for such prominent journals of ideas as the *Nation*, the *New Leader*, and the *Partisan Review*. In 1948 his first major essay, "The Harlem Ghetto," was published in *Commentary* magazine. The essay tackled the difficult and painful issue of the origins of black anti-Semitism, and it caused considerable controversy.

Though he was beginning to establish himself as a writer, Baldwin was exhausted and depressed. He had failed to finish a novel that Wright had urged him to complete, he was not making any money, and he felt alienated in the mostly white community of Greenwich Village. At the end of 1948, he decided to leave the country to live in Paris, France, which black American artists had long regarded as a haven from racial prejudice.

In spite of its reputation as a center of world culture, Paris in 1948 was a bleak city still recovering from the effects of World War II. Baldwin, who had arrived in France with just $40, lived in a series of cheap hotel rooms and at one point even pawned his clothes and his typewriter to pay his bills. He found that when he owed someone money, the supposed French indifference to skin color quickly gave way to intolerance. But gradually he established a circle of friends, one of whom took him to

Switzerland, where in several months he completed his acclaimed first novel, *Go Tell It on the Mountain*, an autobiographical story about a Harlem youth trying to escape the despotism of his stepfather and the suffocating influence of religion. In 1955, he followed with *Notes of a Native Son*, a collection of essays that examine the subtle ways in which racial prejudice damages both blacks and whites. A year later, Dial Press published his second novel, *Giovanni's Room*, a bold exploration of a homosexual relationship. In 1957, eager to take part in the growing civil rights movement and having established himself as a successful writer, Baldwin returned to the United States.

Soon after arriving in the United States, Baldwin toured the South to witness firsthand the wave of sit-ins, demonstrations, boycotts, and marches that were beginning to crack the barriers of discrimination. In Atlanta, Georgia, he met the Reverend Martin Luther King, Jr., and heard him give sermons to black congregations. Overwhelmed by the courage and dedication he saw around him, Baldwin began to write about the ordinary black people who risked beatings and bombings to change their lives. These essays were published in the collection *Nobody Knows My Name: More Notes of a Native Son* in 1961. In 1962, he published his third novel, *Another Country*, which concerned the suicide of jazz drummer Rufus Scott and interracial and bisexual relationships among a circle of friends in Greenwich Village and Harlem. Though controversial, both books were best-sellers.

At this time, Baldwin was becoming more and more involved in the civil rights movement, writing essays and traveling around the country giving lectures on its significance. In 1962, he met Elijah Muhammad, the leader of the Nation of Islam (the so-called Black Muslims), who urged that blacks separate themselves from white society. Though Baldwin himself believed in the integrationist strategy of Martin Luther King, Jr., he was able to understand the forces that drove some blacks to become militant separatists. Out of his experiences with the Black Muslims came *The Fire Next Time*, an apocalyptic vision of the destruction that faced American society if it could not solve its racial problems. The book made Baldwin a national figure and he appeared on the cover of *Time* magazine. In 1963, in the wake of police beatings of civil rights workers in Birmingham, Alabama, Baldwin brought together a group of prominent black artists and educators—including Lena Horne, Harry Belafonte, Lorraine Hansberry, and Kenneth Clark—to urge U.S. attorney general Robert Kennedy to put the full force of the federal government behind new civil rights legislation. On August 28, 1963, he attended the huge "March on Washington for Jobs and Freedom" organized by labor leader A. Philip Randolph and Martin Luther King, Jr., to exert pressure on Congress for a new civil rights bill.

These were heady times for Baldwin. In 1964, he was elected to the National Institute of Arts and Letters. In January 1965, at Cambridge University in England, he won a debate against William F. Buckley of the *National Review* on the need for revolutionary change in American race relations. In March 1965, he joined Martin Luther King, Jr., on his second, successful attempt to march from Selma, Alabama, to Montgomery, Alabama, to pressure President Lyndon Johnson for a new voting-rights act, and he protested America's growing involvement in the war in Vietnam.

At the same time, Baldwin was coming under criticism from more radical black leaders, such as Eldridge Cleaver and Imamu Amiri Baraka, because of his integrationist views and the sympathetic portraits of white characters in some of his works. There were terrible tragedies as well—in the 1960s, Baldwin lived through the assassinations of John and Robert Kennedy, Medgar Evers, and Malcolm X, and in the opinion of several of his friends, he never fully recovered from the murder of Martin Luther King, Jr., in 1968. Despite all this, he refused to abandon his commitment to nonviolent protest and racial harmony.

During the 1970s, Baldwin lived well, even extravagantly, on the income from his books, maintaining residences in New York City, France, and Istanbul, Turkey. He wrote three more novels, *Tell Me How Long the Train's Been Gone*, *If Beale Street Could Talk*, and *Just Above My Head*. He published *A Rap on Race* with anthropologist Margaret Mead, *A Dialogue* with the poet Nikki Giovanni, and a book of essays, *The Devil Finds Work*. But despite this productivity, many critics felt that his creative fire was flickering. In 1981, he traveled to Atlanta, Georgia, to cover the trial of child murderer Wayne Williams for *Playboy* magazine. The resulting essay, "The Evidence of Things Not Seen," raised disturbing questions about the racism that still lingered in American society.

In his last years, Baldwin divided his time between teaching at various American universities and relaxing at his farmhouse in the south of France. In 1986, the French government awarded him the medal of the Legion of Honor. He died in France on December 1, 1987, of cancer. With his bright, wide eyes, his broad grin, his warm, animated face, and his articulate and passionate speaking voice, Baldwin always made a strong impression on those who knew him. In his writing, he always confronted the complex issues of racial and sexual relations with searing honesty and much hope.

CHARLES CHESNUTT

$\mathbf{A}$merica's first published black novelist, Charles Waddell Chesnutt, was born in Cleveland, Ohio, on June 20, 1858. Charles's father, Andrew—the son of a white southern tobacco farmer and his black housekeeper—soon moved his family to Fayetteville, North Carolina, where his own father lived, and opened a grocery store. When Charles was growing up, he spent his free time working in the store, and the countless stories he heard from the customers stayed with him all his life. An avid reader as well as a keen listener, he spent most of his earnings in the local bookstore.

Young Charles was an excellent student, but when he was 14 his father decided that it was time for himto leave school and get a full-time job. Charles went to work for a saloon keeper, but before long his high school principal, Robert Harris, got him a position as a student teacher. Two years later, in 1872, Harris's brother Cicero hired the 16-year-old Chesnutt to be the assistant principal of his school in the city of Charlotte, North Carolina. Chesnutt continued to be a voracious reader, devouring books on literature, history, mathematics, and education. In 1875, feeling lonely while on a teaching assignment in South Carolina, he began to keep a journal in which he developed ideas that would later appear in his writings.

Chesnutt's solitude was to end a year later when he returned to Fayetteville to take a job at the State Colored Normal School, a new college designed to train black teachers. There he met Susan Perry, a Fayetteville native who shared his intellectual interests and greatly admired his energy and accomplishments. The two young teachers began to spend their free time together, and in June 1878, they were married. Their first child, Ethel, was born the following year.

Though he now had much to be pleased about, Chesnutt was deeply troubled by the racial situation in the post–Civil War South. The end of the war and the freeing of the slaves more than a decade earlier had not ushered in an era of social equality; the old injustices remained in slightly less obvious forms. Chesnutt himself, with his fair skin, blue eyes, and brown hair, was in a particularly difficult position. Racist whites still considered him inferior because of his African blood; his fellow blacks, knowing that he could easily "pass" for white whenever he chose, often regarded him as an outsider. Believing that he could escape this dilemma in the North, Chesnutt took leave of his family temporarily in 1878 and traveled to Washington, D.C., in search of work.

Chesnutt could not find a decent job in the nation's capital, and he soon returned to Fayetteville, taking over as principal of the Normal School upon the death of Robert Harris. Shortly thereafter, Susan Chesnutt gave birth to another daughter, Helen. Chesnutt was earning enough to support his growing family in comfort, but his glimpse of life in the big city had left its mark. Chesnutt wanted more than a secure position—he wanted fame, and he wanted to give his children more opportunities than he had enjoyed. The only way to achieve this, he decided, was by establishing himself as a writer. Against the advice of many friends and relatives, Chesnutt again said good-bye to his family and boarded a train for New York City.

Chesnutt had taken great pains to learn the art of shorthand, and his skills as a stenographer earned him a job with a New York financial newspaper. But he soon realized that New York was a very expensive place in which to raise a growing family. (While there, he received news of the birth of a son, Edwin.) Chesnutt then decided on Cleveland, the city of his birth, as the most likely place to settle. He quickly established himself in the midwestern metropolis, working as a stenographer in a judge's office and studying law at night. In 1884, he was finally able to send for his family.

Throughout his time in Cleveland, Chesnutt had worked on his writing whenever possible, refining his skills and hoping for a break. His opportunity arrived in the form of a story contest sponsored by S. S. McClure's newspaper syndicate. Chesnutt submitted a story entitled "Uncle Peter's House," and although he did not win the contest, the story impressed McClure, who bought it for $10 and then resold it to a Cleveland newspaper.

Published in 1885, Chesnutt's story was the first work of fiction in decades to depict blacks as ordinary human beings rather than scoundrels or likeable fools. In the two years following his breakthrough, Chesnutt sold seven more stories to McClure, published a number of poems and sketches in various magazines, and passed the Ohio bar exam with the highest score among all the applicants.

When one of Chesnutt's stories was published in the influential *Atlantic Monthly*, he began to attract a wider following. In addition to his stories, he also published essays on the racial situation in the South. Before long, his fiction began to deal almost exclusively with racial themes.

Despite his success in selling his stories and his flourishing stenographic practice, Chesnutt was still dogged by an unfulfilled ambition—he wanted to see a book with his name on it. It took him nearly a decade to achieve this goal, but at last, in March 1899, the distinguished Boston firm of Houghton Mifflin and Company brought out *The Conjure Woman*, a collection of Chesnutt's stories retelling the tales of African sorcery he had absorbed during his days in the South.

Chesnutt's first book broke the dam. Within the space of a year, he found publishers for two other works, a biography of the antislavery activist Frederick Douglass and a second book of fiction, *The Wife of His Youth and Other Stories of the Color Line*. In this story collection, Chesnutt explored his most important theme, the fate of mixed-bloods in a racist society. Many reviewers—among them William Dean Howells, the nation's most influential man of letters—praised Chesnutt's writings for their quality and their subject matter. But in the straitlaced atmosphere of the age, others condemned his frank treatment of racial issues, especially the intermarriage of whites and blacks. Nevertheless, Chesnutt made an indelible mark on the literary scene—by publishing a book of fiction, he had achieved something no other black American had previously been able to accomplish.

Never afraid to take risks, Chesnutt decided in 1899 to abandon his stenographic business and devote himself completely to writing. His faith in his ability was quickly rewarded, for in the following year Houghton Mifflin decided to publish his first novel, *The House*

Behind the Cedars. Though the book's treatment of racial issues again aroused resistance and held down sales, the publishers were committed to Chesnutt. In 1901, they published his second novel, *The Marrow of Tradition*, which was based on a race riot that had taken place in North Carolina three years earlier. Predictably, the book was violently condemned in the South and praised in the North. When sales fell far short of the 20,000 copies the publishers had hoped for, Chesnutt reopened his stenography business. By any standard, he was a successful man. His daughters were educated at Smith College and his son at Harvard University, and in 1904 he moved his family into a spacious home on one of Cleveland's most appealing residential avenues.

As racial questions began to be discussed with more candor and urgency in the early years of the 20th century, Chesnutt's voice was one of the most eloquent to be raised in support of social and political equality. By the 1920s, when black culture began to emerge in a burst of pride and artistic achievement, Chesnutt was the dean of African American literature, respected by the younger generation as well as his own. In 1928, the 70-year-old author was awarded the Spingarn Medal by the National Association for the Advancement of Colored People (NAACP) in recognition of all his varied achievements.

Energized by the award and the praise it brought him, Chesnutt set to work on a new novel, entitled *The Quarry*. Unfortunately, Chesnutt's writing style was out of step with the times, which demanded more realism than romanticism, and the book was turned down by publishers.

Disappointed but not discouraged, Chesnutt continued to maintain his lively interest in a variety of subjects and to enjoy his hobby of fly-fishing, which he indulged at his family's summer retreat in Michigan. In 1932 his health began to fail, and upon returning from the office one afternoon he was forced to take to his bed. Four days later, on November 15, he died painlessly in the presence of his wife and daughters. Through his energy and courage, Charles Chesnutt advanced the still-unrealized goal of a just society, one in which, in his words, "men will be esteemed and honored for their character and their talents."

PAUL LAURENCE DUNBAR

The first black American to gain international recognition as a poet and novelist, Paul Laurence Dunbar was born on June 27, 1872, in Dayton, Ohio. His father, Joshua Dunbar, had been a slave on a Kentucky farm until he escaped to Canada and freedom by the Underground Railroad. During the Civil War, he returned to the United States and joined the all-black 55th Massachusetts

Infantry Regiment and fought with distinction near Jacksonville, Florida, and Charleston, South Carolina, rising to the rank of sergeant. After the war, remembering the kindness shown him as a fugitive slave by the people of Ohio, he moved to Dayton. Paul's mother, Matilda, was also a slave, a domestic servant on a Kentucky farm who had been sold away from her family when still a child. She tried to run away in 1863, but while on the run she heard about President Abraham Lincoln's Emancipation Proclamation and returned to the farm to await the Union victory. After the war, widowed with two children, she moved to Dayton, Ohio, where she met and married Joshua Dunbar. His parents never let Paul forget that he was one of the first generation of black Americans born in freedom.

Paul's parents divorced when he was still young, but they continued to live near each other and both took an interest in his education. Dunbar excelled in all-black elementary schools and at the age of 12 began to show an interest in writing poetry. "I rhymed continually," he said, "trying to put together words with a jingling sound." In 1885, he entered an all-white Dayton high school, but he continued to do well and had no difficulty making friends and winning the respect of his fellow students. One of his close friends was Orville Wright, who with his brother Wilbur would go on to invent the airplane. At the time, the Wright brothers were thinking of going into the bicycle business, and they had also built their own printing press and were publishing a local newspaper, the *West Side News*. Dunbar wrote articles for the paper, and soon the Wrights were also printing the *Dayton Tattler*, aimed at the town's black readership and edited and almost entirely written by Dunbar.

After graduation, Dunbar tried to get a job as a reporter for one of Dayton's newspapers, but he quickly discovered that black journalists were not in demand. Instead, he went to work as an elevator operator in a local bank building, but his poems, published in the newspapers that would not hire him, began to attract attention beyond Dayton, and Orville Wright urged him to publish a collection of his works in book form. In 1892, encouraged by a letter of admiration from the esteemed poet James Whitcomb Riley, he published at his own expense an anthology of 56 poems under the title *Oak and Ivy*. Dunbar wrote in the romantic, lyrical style of his favorite poets, Percy Bysshe Shelley, John Keats, and Alfred Lord Tennyson, but he celebrated the nobility of ordinary people leading ordinary lives, and he successfully captured the sounds and rhythms of black speech. Many of the poems were nostalgic in tone and looked back toward a simpler country life, a popular theme in the post–Civil War period of industrial expansion and rapid change.

Dunbar's reputation began to grow, and in 1893 the editors of the *Dayton Herald* asked him to go to Chicago to report on the nation's first World's Fair, the World's Columbian Exposition. In Chicago, he worked briefly as a secretary for the fiery anti-slavery activist Frederick Douglass, recently retired as foreign minister to Haiti. The experience encouraged Dunbar to seek a wider audience for his work and to write more poems dealing with the struggle for racial equality.

The Wrights printed a flier for him, advertising his skills as a poet and lecturer, and Dunbar began to give poetry readings in many cities. He worked briefly as a law clerk for a prominent Dayton attorney but soon found that the work interfered with his writing and abandoned it. In 1894, the prestigious literary magazine *Century* published three of his poems, and he determined to find some way to make a living as a poet. In 1896, he published a second anthology of poetry, *Majors and Minors*, which was favorably reviewed by the novelist William Dean Howells in *Harper's Weekly*, bringing Dunbar to national attention. According to Howells, Dunbar was "so far as I know, the first man of his color to study his race objectively, to analyze it to himself, and then to represent it in art as he felt it and found it to be; to represent it humorously, yet tenderly, and above all so faithfully that we know the portrait to be undeniably like . . . intellectually Dunbar makes a stronger claim for the Negro than any Negro has yet done."

In the summer of 1896, Dunbar traveled to New York City to meet Howells, who was then regarded as America's foremost man of letters. While there, he signed a contract with Dodd, Mead & Company for his third anthology, *Lyrics of Lowly Life*, which gained him an international reputation as a poet. In 1897, he traveled to London, where he met the black composer Samuel Coleridge-Taylor, and the two men collaborated on a number of choral works that set Dunbar's poetry to music. In 1898, he returned to the United States, married the poet Alice Ruth Moore, and accepted a position as an assistant librarian at the Library of Congress in Washington, D.C. He worked with the black musician Will Marion Cook on *Clorindy*, a musical about the popular dance craze the cakewalk, wrote a volume of short stories about the Deep South entitled *Folks from Dixie*, and published his first novel, *The Uncalled*. But one of the main characters of *The Uncalled* was a white man, and critics attacked Dunbar for not sticking to what he knew best—the lives of black folk. Angry that he was being narrowly defined as a black writer, Dunbar began to speak and write more forcefully about racism and prejudice in American society.

In 1899, Dunbar published his fourth book of poetry, *Lyrics of the Hearthside*, but he found himself increasingly bothered by a hacking cough that would not go away. Widely heralded as the "poet laureate of the Negro race," he gave up his job with the Library of Congress and tried to support himself with lecture tours and poetry readings, but his health did not improve. In April 1899, while in New York City on his way to Albany to meet with Governor Theodore Roosevelt, he collapsed in Grand Central Terminal. He was diagnosed as suffering from pneumonia and underwent a long period of recuperation in the Catskill Mountains of upstate New York and in Denver, Colorado, but his real ailment—

tuberculosis—had been misdiagnosed, and he never fully recovered.

Though Dunbar cut down on his poetry readings and speaking engagements, he continued to write. In 1901 and 1902 he completed two novels, *The Fanatics* and *The Sport of the Gods*, both of which, unlike some of his earlier sentimental writing, took a harsher and more realistic look at race relations in the United States. These books were pioneering works that would greatly influence Claude McKay, James Weldon Johnson, Langston Hughes, and other young black writers of the Harlem Renaissance of the 1920s and encourage them to speak bluntly about problems of race.

By 1903, Dunbar's already precarious health had been further undermined by a drinking problem, which was aggravated by his doctors' prescription of wine and whiskey to treat his respiratory problems. He had separated from his wife and returned to live with his mother in Dayton, Ohio. He had witnessed race riots and subtle forms of segregation in northern cities, and his writings grew angrier and more despairing. He published several more collections of poetry—*Lyrics of Love and Laughter* and *Lyrics of Sunshine and Shadow* in 1903 and *L'il' Gal* in 1904—that revealed the poet's darker mood, but his energies were waning. "Something within me seems to be dead," he said. "There is not spirit or energy left in me."

Upset at the breakup of his marriage, at his publishers (who seemed only to want more verse in black dialect), and at his own failing health, Paul Laurence

Dunbar died of tuberculosis on February 9, 1906. He was survived by his mother, who lived to the age of 95 in the house that is now a public museum dedicated to the poet. His *Complete Poems* was published posthumously in 1913. Though his style of poetry is unfashionable today, Paul Laurence Dunbar was the first black writer to be accepted as an American man of letters and the first to teach that the lives of black people were an integral part of the American experience.

RALPH ELLISON

The author of one of the most important American novels of the 20th century, Ralph Waldo Ellison was born on March 1, 1914, in Oklahoma City, Oklahoma. At the turn of the century, Oklahoma was a new, sparsely settled territory, and Ralph's parents, along with thousands of other black Americans, had migrated there from the Deep South in search of a better way of life. Ralph's father, Lewis

Ellison, had high hopes for his son and named him after the 19th-century poet and philosopher Ralph Waldo Emerson, whose notion of "self-reliance" seemed to the father the key to success. Lewis Ellison died three years after his oldest son was born; after reading several of Emerson's works in school, Ralph, unduly burdened by his father's expectations, refused to use his middle name and vowed never to read Emerson again.

After the death of his father, Ralph's mother, Ida, worked as a maid and building superintendent to support Ralph and his younger brother. She brought home old books, magazines, and records to encourage her children's interests in whatever fascinated them. "They spoke to me of a life which was broader and more interesting," Ellison said of the things his mother brought him, "and although it was not really a part of my own life, I never thought they were not for me simply because I happened to be a Negro. They were things which spoke of a world I could someday make my own." One of Ralph's first loves was music. He worked in a drugstore where local jazz musicians often came by, and at Douglass High School he learned to play the trumpet and the saxophone. From his mother's African Methodist Episcopalian church he learned black spirituals and hymns, and he dreamed of becoming a musician and composing a symphony.

In 1933, Ellison received a state scholarship to study music at the prestigious all-black Tuskegee Institute in Alabama. Ellison was never comfortable at Tuskegee, and he could not adjust to the intense racial segregation off campus. But while there, he developed an interest in literature, discovering the modernists of the world literary scene—Ernest Hemingway, T. S. Eliot, Ezra Pound, and James Joyce. He perceived in the works of these writers new rhythms and a new use of language that reminded him of jazz and could be adapted to express the black experience. In Ellison's third year at Tuskegee there was a problem with his scholarship, and in the spring of 1936 he decided to go to New York City, partly to earn the money to continue school and partly to experience the cultural life of the city's famous black community, Harlem.

In the 1920s, a new generation of black writers, musicians, and artists launched the Harlem Renaissance, exploring the black experience with a new intellectual freedom, supported by a large, sophisticated urban black audience. By the time Ellison arrived in New York City in 1936, the Great Depression had sapped some of Harlem's vitality, but it was still a stimulating environment for a would-be artist, and such prominent black writers as W. E. B. Du Bois and Arna Bontemps were still active. "I thought of it," Ellison said, "as the freest of American cities and considered Harlem as the site and symbol of Afro-American progress." Ellison studied briefly with the black sculptor Augusta Savage and met the novelist Richard Wright and the poet Langston Hughes, who introduced him to the politically engaged novels of the French writer André Malraux.

To this point in his life, Ellison had planned on becoming a composer, but his new friendships, especially with Wright, gradually convinced him to make literature his vocation. "He had as much curiosity about how writing is written as I had about how music is composed," Ellison later wrote about Wright, "and our curiosity concerning artistic creation became the basis of our friendship." When an audition for Duke Ellington's Orchestra failed to work out, Ellison gave up music and any plans to return to Tuskegee, now determined to become a writer. "My ambitions as a composer had been fatally diverted," Wright later said about this period of his life.

In 1938, Ellison went to work for the Federal Writers' Project, a division of the Works Progress Administration (WPA), a depression-era program designed to alleviate unemployment. His assignment was to interview hundreds of black New Yorkers and help prepare a living history of their experiences. In 1939, he began to publish short stories. In 1942, he left the Federal Writers' Project to become managing editor of the new radical magazine *Negro Quarterly.* Many young black artists of the period were attracted to the radical ideas of the Communist party, but when the party, during World War II, refused to protest segregated army units, Ellison lost interest in the organization. In 1943, he joined the racially mixed merchant marine and worked for two years as a ship's cook and baker, continuing to write stories throughout the war. In 1946, he married Fanny

McConnell, a Fisk University graduate with a strong interest in his writing.

After the war, Ellison began to work seriously on the novel that would make him famous, *Invisible Man*. Parts of the book were published in British and American literary magazines as early as 1947, but the finished novel was first published in 1952. *Invisible Man* is an allegory, a symbolic story deeply influenced by surrealist trends in modern European literature. It tells of an unnamed southern black youth trying to survive in a world of white hypocrisy that denies him a sense of individual identity. Forced to compete in a world where whites make the rules and blackness must be denied, the hero comes to think of himself as "invisible," a nonperson not only to others but to himself. "At first you tell yourself it's all a dirty joke, or that it's due to the 'political situation,'" Ellison's narrator explains, "but deep down you come to suspect that you've yourself to blame, and you stand naked and shivering before the millions of eyes who look through you unseeingly."

Ellison hoped that the novel would speak as profoundly to whites as it did to blacks. "I conceived of the novel," he said, "as an account, on the specific level, of a young Negro American's experience. But I hoped at the same time to write so well that anyone who shared everything except his racial identity could identify with it, because there was never any questions in my mind that Negroes were human, and thus being human, their experience became metaphors for the experiences of other people."

Invisible Man was an immediate success, and in 1953 it won the National Book Award, making Ellison the first black writer so honored. In 1955, Ellison received a fellowship from the American Academy of Arts and Letters and spent two years in Rome, Italy, trying to write a second novel on similar themes. When the novel simply would not come together, he published various parts of it as short stories. In 1964, he published *Shadow and Act*, a collection of essays on how deeply all of American culture had been influenced by the black experience. During the 1960s, an increasingly militant civil rights movement, embittered by the assassinations of its leaders and anxious to build a separate black culture, turned away from Ellison, who was steadfast in his refusal to adopt political labels. He saw the black struggle for racial equality as a uniquely American experience, for example, and showed little interest in its African roots. But *Invisible Man* continued to sell and has not been out of print since it first appeared.

In the late 1960s, Ellison began to lecture at major American universities. He and his wife bought an old farm in Plainfield, Massachusetts, hoping to retire to the country. But in 1967 the farm burned down, destroying much of his work in progress. In 1970, he received a literary award from the French government, which was presented to him by the writer who had so excited him as a young man, André Malraux, who was now the French minister of cultural affairs. In 1975, he returned to Oklahoma City for the dedication of the Ralph Ellison Branch Library. He received several honorary degrees and participated in many arts councils and foundations that created opportunities for new black artists. In 1985, Ellison published *Going to the Territory*, another collection of essays about the nature of American literature and artists such as Richard Wright and Duke Ellington. Ellison continues to act as a spokesman for black artists, but always on his own terms. "My problem was that I always tried to go in everyone's way but my own," Ellison had written in *Invisible Man*. "I have also been called one thing and then another while no one really wished to hear what I called myself. So after years of trying to adopt the opinions of others I finally rebelled."

ALEX HALEY

A lex Haley, who electrified the American public with his award-winning family saga, *Roots*, was born on August 11, 1921, in Ithaca, New York. At the time of his birth, his parents, Simon Haley and Bertha Palmer Haley, were both graduate students. Because it was difficult for the young parents to care for an infant while pursuing their education, they brought baby Alex to Henning, Tennessee, so that he could be cared for by his maternal grandparents, Will and Cynthia Palmer.

The family was eventually reunited, but when Alex was 10, his mother died. Simon Haley, now a college dean, carried on as best he could and pushed his children to excel, but his message was not well received by Alex, who missed his mother and resented his father for remarrying after two years. Though he was bright enough to graduate from high school and enter college at the age of 15, Alex had no idea what he wanted to do with his life. After two years of study, he dropped out and enlisted in the U.S. Coast Guard for a three-year hitch.

In the Coast Guard, Haley was assigned to a cargo-ammunition ship on duty in the Southwest Pacific, where he served first as a messboy and then as a cook. Bored by the long periods of inactivity common in shipboard life, Haley read everything in the ship's library and wrote long letters to all of his friends and relatives. When his shipmates discovered that Haley had a way with words, he began tapping out love letters to women all over the globe on his small portable typewriter. Having started in this vein, Haley began to write sentimental love stories, which he hoped to sell to various romance magazines. The editors sent back a steady stream of rejection slips, but Haley had begun to think of himself as a writer.

The Coast Guard made use of Haley's writing skills by shifting him to a public relations job in New York City. While writing speeches for other officers, he grew interested in the history of the Coast Guard and began to write adventure stories based on the yarns he had heard from former shipmates. When three of these pieces were accepted by *Coronet* magazine, Haley's literary fortunes took a major turn for the better.

In the end, Haley's 3-year hitch in the Coast Guard turned into a full 20-year career. When he retired from the service in 1959, he applied for work with a number of advertising and public relations firms in New York. Though he had first-rate qualifications, it became clear that big-time public relations was a whites-only affair. Haley then decided to go for broke: he found a dingy one-room apartment in Greenwich Village and spent all his waking hours at the typewriter.

The determined author endured some hard times ("One day I was down to 18 cents and a can of sardines," he later recalled), but by the end of the year the popular magazine *Reader's Digest* commissioned him to write a series of celebrity profiles. This led to an assignment from *Playboy*, the successful men's magazine, for a series of interviews with notable African Americans. Haley proved to be highly adept in this forum, and his lengthy conversations with such important figures as Miles Davis, Jim Brown, and Leontyne Price were a great hit with the magazine's editors and readers.

The turning point in Haley's career came in 1962 when *Playboy* suggested that he interview the controversial Black Muslim minister Malcolm X. Haley, who had first met Malcolm in 1959, had a difficult time gaining the militant leader's trust, but when the interview was finally published, its uncensored presentation of Malcolm's fiery antiwhite and anti-Christian views caused a national sensation. As a result, Haley was approached by Grove Press with the proposal that he do a full-length book on Malcolm.

Reluctantly at first and then with great frankness, Malcolm told Haley the story of his life in a series of long conversations, describing his progress, under the influence of the Nation of Islam, from street criminal to civil rights activist. As the book developed, it charted Malcolm's evolution toward a more universal view of race relations and his growing estrangement from the Nation of Islam. Just two weeks after the completion of the manuscript, Malcolm was assassinated by Black Muslim gunmen in New York City. Published in 1966, *The Autobiography of Malcolm X, As Told to Alex Haley* was immediately recognized as a unique document of a remarkable American life.

One of the things Haley had learned from Malcolm X was the necessity for African Americans to take pride in their identity and their history. Recalling all the stories he had been told as a boy about his own family's experiences, Haley resolved to turn these recollections into a book. He soon interested Doubleday, one of the nation's leading publishers, in the project, and received a $5,000 advance. He expected to have a manuscript in a year's time.

As Haley worked on the book, however, he was drawn deeper and deeper into the past, puzzled by certain unintelligible words his grandmother had used in her stories. After consulting scholars, he learned that these words derived from the Mandingo language of West Africa, and he decided that he could not tell his family's story without delving into its African origins.

After securing a grant from his old employers at *Reader's Digest*, Haley traveled to Africa and painstakingly tracked down a tribal historian, or griot, in a small village on the Gambia River. After the elderly griot had recited various incidents of tribal history for two hours, he mentioned a man named Kunta Kinte, who had disappeared from the village a long time before, shortly after the "King's soldiers" came to the village from abroad.

Haley was electrified. Kunta Kinte was the same man his grandmother had told him about, the ancestor who had been taken from his country by slave traders and brought to America in chains.

Deeply moved and excited by his discovery, Haley also understood the enormous labor involved in reconstructing the saga of Kunta Kinte and his descendants in the New World. He began by taking a freighter from Gambia to the United States, trying to relive the journey of the slave ship, and went on to talk with thousands of people and visit more than 50 libraries and archives throughout the world. Finally, in February 1976—10 years past its original due date—Haley delivered his manuscript to the editors at Doubleday.

The wait was worth it, both for the publishers and for Haley. *Roots: The Saga of an American Family* appeared in the nation's bookstores on September 17 and became an instant sensation. By the end of the year, more than 500,000 copies were in print, and ABC television had signed a deal to produce a 12-hour miniseries based on the book. The agreement included a payment to Haley of $1 million, a staggering fee for an author at that time.

The money did not immediately change the simple life-style of the 55-year-old Haley, but when ABC aired "Roots," he soon became a public figure of major proportions. The miniseries, aired on six successive evenings, was watched by 90 million viewers, the largest audience for a single program in television history. Boosted by the success of the program and the sequel that aired a year later, Haley's book was translated into 31 languages and sold more than 8 million copies worldwide. The author was showered with awards, citations, and honorary degrees, capped by a special Pulitzer Prize awarded him in 1977 for his "important contribution to the history of slavery."

Unfortunately, Haley soon learned that celebrity has its drawbacks. Following Haley's Pulitzer Prize, critics began to attack the historical validity of *Roots*. Haley had quite candidly stated that although the dates and major events in his book were accurate, he had made up incidents and dialogue in order to flesh out the story. Nevertheless, he was sued by two prominent black novelists who claimed that he had improperly used passages from their work. One suit was dismissed; in the other case, Haley decided to make an out-of-court settlement, against the advice of his publishers.

Haley was deeply hurt by the accusations, and his search for personal contentment continued to be a difficult one. His lifelong devotion to writing had caused three marriages to end in divorce; aside from meeting the countless people inspired by *Roots*, his main enjoyment derived from entertaining friends at the splendid estate he had bought in Tennessee.

By the 1990s, Haley found the time to begin another serious project, this one centering on an ancestor who was a slave owner of Irish descent. A television version of the story "Queenie" was broadcast with great fanfare in 1993, but the novel remained unfinished—Alex Haley had died of a heart attack on February 10, 1992. Though his final years were troubled by controversy, he will always be remembered for inspiring black Americans with a new sense of pride in their heritage.

CHESTER HIMES

Criminal, convict, black protest writer, and master of the detective novel, Chester Bomar Himes was born on July 29, 1909, in Jefferson City, Missouri, the youngest of three brothers. His father, Joseph, was a skilled blacksmith and wheelwright who taught at Lincoln Institute. His mother, Estelle, was also a teacher. In 1919, Chester's father accepted a teaching position at Alcorn A. & M.

College and moved his family to Alcorn, Mississippi, a move that appalled his wife because it exposed the family to the institutionalized segregation of the Deep South. Believing that Mississippi's segregated schools were worthless, Chester's mother, who was light-skinned and often passed as white, tutored him at home. One night, as a gesture of protest, she checked into a whites-only hotel; the scandal that resulted when she announced in the morning that she was black cost Chester's father his job and forced the family to leave town.

The Himes family settled first in Pine Bluff, Arkansas, where an accident in a high school chemistry lab blinded Himes's brother, Joe. The family then moved to St. Louis, Missouri, to obtain better medical treatment for Joe. In 1923, the family moved again, this time to Cleveland, Ohio. After graduating from high school, Himes went to work as a busboy in a hotel to save money for college, but he was seriously injured when he fell down the hotel's elevator shaft. After being denied treatment at a whites-only hospital, he suffered through a long and painful recovery. In 1926, he finally enrolled at Ohio State University in Columbus, but he could not adjust to the segregated life on campus and did poorly. At the end of his first year, at the age of 18, he dropped out of school.

With his parents continually fighting and his home life in disarray, Himes spent his time in the streets and fell in with the Cleveland underworld. He became involved in gambling, prostitution, check forging, and the illegal sale of liquor. He began to carry a gun. In late 1928, he broke into a house and stole some jewelry. He was arrested, tried, and sentenced to 25 years of hard labor at the Ohio State Penitentiary. In prison, Himes started to write short stories to pass the time. They were cynical stories of criminals and convicts trapped by their circumstances and driven to commit acts of violence. In 1934, two of his stories, "Crazy in the Stir" and "To What Red Hell," were published by *Esquire* magazine under the byline "Prisoner No. 59623."

In 1936, after seven years in jail, Himes was paroled. He came out of the penitentiary in the middle of the Great Depression, and work was hard to find. In 1937, he married his longtime girlfriend, Jean Johnson, and took a succession of jobs as a waiter and bellhop at several Cleveland hotels and country clubs as he tried to support himself as a writer. More of his stories were published by *Esquire* and *The Crisis*, the journal of the National Association for the Advancement of Colored People (NAACP), but there was little money to be made. In 1943, at the suggestion of the poet Langston Hughes, Himes went to Los Angeles to try to write for Hollywood, but in the film industry blacks were wanted only for menial labor. He got a job in the Los Angeles shipyards and after hours began to work on his first novel. During a three-year period, while continuing to write short stories, essays, and his novel, Himes held 23 different jobs.

In 1944, Doubleday published Himes's *If He Hollers Let Him Go*, a bitter novel about a black man in Los Angeles tormented by a series of racial incidents.

Though unrelentingly harsh in its depiction of race relations, the book was well received. Himes moved to New York and in 1947 finished *Lonely Crusade*, another novel, this time about a black union organizer who is betrayed by everyone he relies upon. *Lonely Crusade* was too harsh for the critics, however, who attacked it ruthlessly, for Himes's unrelenting portrayal of the effects of racial oppression on black Americans made both black and white readers profoundly uneasy. "If this plumbing for the truth reveals within the Negro personality homicidal mania," he said in a 1948 speech, "a pathetic sense of inferiority . . . arrogance, Uncle Tomism, hate and fear and self-hate, this then is the effect of oppression on the human personality. These are the daily horrors, the daily realities, the daily experiences of an oppressed minority."

In 1948, Himes briefly became a writer-in-residence at the Yaddo artists' retreat in Saratoga Springs, New York, but he was depressed by the negative reaction to *Lonely Crusade* and had difficulty writing while there. He managed to complete two autobiographical novels, *Cast the First Stone* and *The Third Generation*, but could not find publishers for them until the early 1950s. His marriage began to deteriorate, and Himes started to drink and use drugs so heavily that he experienced frequent extended blackouts.

In 1953, Himes decided that he could escape all his troubles by leaving the United States. In April of that year, following the path taken by his friend, the expatriate writer Richard Wright, Himes sailed for Paris. Wright helped him find a room across from the Café Tournon, a popular meeting place for black intellectuals. Himes met James Baldwin and other black writers, but the constant discussions about race depressed him, and in July 1953, he moved to London. He was now living with Alva Trent, a Dutch woman he had met on the way to Europe. In January 1955, Himes and Trent returned to the United States briefly and settled in Greenwich Village in New York City. Himes had been writing novels and short stories throughout this period, but they had been rejected by publishers as too violent and melodramatic, and he was now reduced to washing dishes and mopping floors in Horn & Hardart Automats to support himself. In December 1955, he returned to Paris alone, determined to find a new and more successful direction for his fiction.

"I [still] had the creative urge," he later said about that period in his life, "but the old, used forms for the black American writer did not fit my creations. I wanted to break through the barriers that labeled me as a protest writer. I knew the life of an American black needed another image than just the victim of racism. We were more than just victims. We did not suffer, we were extroverts. We were unique individuals, funny but not clowns, solemn but not serious, hurt but not suffering . . . we had a tremendous love of life."

At the request of the French publisher Gallimard, Himes abandoned his role as a black protest writer and turned to detective stories. He studied the works of

Dashiell Hammett and Raymond Chandler and began to produce a series of novels and stories based
on the exploits of two fictional black detectives in
Harlem, Grave Digger Jones and Coffin Ed Johnson.
The violent, melodramatic style that had frightened
the critics of his earlier works seemed to work per-
fectly in his crime fiction. In 1957, one of his first
efforts, *The Five-Cornered Square,* was chosen by the
French as the best detective novel of the year. In 1964,
he completed *Cotton Comes to Harlem,* another detective novel that was in part a satire of the "Back to
Africa" movement of the black nationalist leader Mar-
cus Garvey, a notion that Himes regarded, in the past
and in the present, as absurd. "The American black
man has to make it or lose it in America; he has no
choice," he said.

Himes was enjoying renewed popularity in France,
but in the United States his books were usually published in cheap paperback editions with altered titles
and mangled texts. In 1965, in France, where he was,
he said, "the best-known black in Paris," he married
Leslie Packard, a columnist for the Paris edition of the
New York *Herald Tribune.*

In 1967, Himes completed *Blind Man with a Pistol,*
an unusual detective story that condemned the cruel-
ties and absurdities of life in Harlem and drew no
simple conclusions. In 1970, Samuel Goldwyn, Jr.,
released the film version of *Cotton Comes to Harlem,*
and Himes's reputation in the United States finally
began to grow. In 1972 and 1974, Himes published
two volumes of autobiography, *The Quality of Hurt*

and *My Life of Absurdity*. By the 1980s, he was suffering from Parkinson's disease, and on November 12, 1984, at the age of 75, he died in Moraira, Spain.

There had been many ironies in Himes's life. He had gone from petty criminal to prison convict to an internationally recognized author of crime fiction that was often based on his personal experiences. As a protest writer, his unflinching portrayal of the violence in the lives of black Americans had angered critics, but the same world of violence had proved acceptable within the context of detective fiction. He had left the United States seeking peace of mind and acceptance of his work, but he could never turn away from the source of his stories—the black ghettos of America—and he always believed that the future of blacks lay in the struggle for equality at home, not in running away to Africa or Europe.

LANGSTON HUGHES

A merica's preeminent black poet and a leading figure of the Harlem Renaissance, James Langston Hughes was born on February 1, 1902, in Joplin, Missouri. His parents' marriage was not a happy one, and they separated when Langston was very young. He spent much of his youth in Lawrence, Kansas, in the care of his grandmother, a strong-willed, religious woman who had been married to one of the men who died with John Brown at Harpers Ferry. As a child of a broken home, Langston grew up feeling a strong sense of isolation and loneliness. Unlike his grandmother, he found no consolation in religion.

In 1916, Hughes entered Central High School in Cleveland, Ohio. There, he began to find pleasure in books and literature. He developed an interest in poetry and wrote poems for the school magazine, copying the broad cadences and free verse of his favorite poets, Walt Whitman and Carl Sandburg. But from the beginning, his poems revealed an individual genius with bursts of song from black spirituals, blues and jazz rhythms, and a language enriched by regional black dialects.

After graduation, Hughes dreamed of attending Columbia University in New York City. When he was summoned to Toluca, Mexico, by his father, he went, hoping to get the money for his college education. James Hughes, however, wanted his son to become a mining engineer and refused him the money. Hughes then stayed in Mexico, working as a teacher and continuing to write poetry. In 1920, he sent several poems, including "The Negro Speaks of Rivers," to two of Harlem's most well known magazines, the arts journal *Brownie's Book* and *Crisis*, the magazine of the National Association for the Advancement of Colored People (NAACP), edited by W. E. B. Du Bois. The poems were published and, seeing his son's success, Hughes's father relented and agreed to finance his first year at Columbia.

Hughes arrived in New York in September 1921. He did not enjoy his year at Columbia, however. His classes bored him, and there were very few black students at the university. He preferred the city's entertainments—Harlem jazz clubs, Broadway plays by such playwrights as Eugene O'Neill and George Bernard Shaw, and new productions by left-wing theater groups. When his first year at Columbia was finished, he left school and moved to Harlem. He met Du Bois and the younger black intellectuals grouped around the NAACP and was encouraged to continue with his poetry. In early 1923, he wrote "The Weary Blues," a brilliant evocation of black speech and music, a pioneering effort in the creation of a new poetic voice for African Americans.

As more of his poems appeared in Du Bois's *Crisis*, Hughes began to attract a growing readership, but he was restless. In the summer of 1923, he took a job as a seaman aboard an old freighter, the *West Hesseltine*, and sailed to Africa. He marveled at the vitality and diversity of African tribal culture, but he also saw how the continent was exploited and impoverished by the European colonial powers. In late 1923, he shipped out again aboard the *McKeesport*, this time bound for Europe. He made his way to Paris, where he got a job as a dishwasher at Le Grand Duc, a popular nightclub. After hours, jazz musicians would come into the club for late-night jam sessions. The Parisians seemed free of prejudice against blacks, and everywhere there was artistic experimentation and excitement. In 1924, Hughes moved on to Italy, where he was stranded in Genoa without enough money to return home. Depressed and homesick, he wrote one of his most famous poems, "I, Too, Sing America," echoing the words of Walt Whitman and insisting that the black man be free to "sit at the table" with other Americans. Finally, Hughes found a ship to take him home. He had arrived in Paris with seven dollars in his pocket and returned to the United States with 25 cents. He jokingly said that his grand tour of Europe had cost him "exactly six dollars and seventy-five cents."

By the time Hughes returned home in late 1924, the publication of his poems in leading black journals had established him as a major artist of the Harlem Renaissance. But Hughes chose not to stay in Harlem. Instead, he moved to Washington, D.C., in 1925 to reunite with his mother. During this time, he wrote "Railroad Avenue" and "The Cat and the Saxophone," two poems that imposed violent jazz rhythms on verse. His works were now appearing in *Vanity Fair*, and Alfred Knopf agreed to publish his first collection of poems under the title *The Weary Blues*. In late 1925, while working as a busboy in a downtown Washington hotel, he slipped several of his works to the poet Vachel Lindsay, who had come in for dinner before giving a poetry reading. Later at the poetry reading, Lindsay announced that he had "discovered" a talented new black poet and read Hughes's poems along with his own. The incident helped Hughes find a larger audience outside of the black community.

In 1926, Hughes enrolled at Lincoln University, an all-black college near Philadelphia, Pennsylvania. When he was not studying, Hughes would travel up to Harlem to meet with a small circle of black artists whom the writer Zora Neale Hurston had named the Niggerati. In 1927, Knopf published his second collection of poetry under the title *Fine Clothes for the Jew*. He met Charlotte Mason, a wealthy New York widow, who helped to support him for three years. He graduated from Lincoln University in 1929, the year the Great Depression hit the country. In 1930, he published *Not Without Laughter*, an autobiographical novel about his childhood.

During the 1930s, Hughes became more radical politically, writing poems that protested racial and social injustice, and supporting many of the causes of the Communist party. He toured the South giving poetry readings, and in 1932 he traveled to the former Soviet Union. He returned to the United States and settled in Carmel, California, an artists' colony where a friend had offered him a rent-free cottage in which he could write. He joined the local branch of the John Reed Club, a group of left-wing artists, and became involved in supporting strikes by farm workers and longshoremen. In 1934, he published a collection of stories entitled *The Ways of White Folks*. But as his views became more radical, his audience outside the black community declined, and many of his works were turned down by publishers.

In late 1934, after a brief trip to Mexico to settle the estate of his deceased father, Hughes returned to

New York to work on several plays. *Mulatto*, *Troubled Island*, and *Joy to My Soul* were produced on Broadway in the late 1930s. In 1937, Hughes returned to Paris, where he was drawn into the Alliance of Antifascist Intellectuals, an organization that was formed to save Republican Spain from the right-wing rebellion of Francisco Franco. Hughes traveled to Spain and toured the battlefronts of the Spanish civil war as a reporter for the Baltimore *Afro-American* and the Associated Press. He came into close contact with other antifascist artists such as André Malraux, Ernest Hemingway, Lillian Hellman, and Dorothy Parker.

Hughes returned to New York in 1938 and produced the play *Don't You Want To Be Free?* for the Harlem Suitcase Theater, which he had cofounded with Louise Thompson. He tried writing for Hollywood but found the experience humiliating. No matter what he wrote, the film industry twisted it to fit its primitive stereotypes of black people. By 1942, he was back in Harlem, working for the Writers War Board with W. C. Handy, producing patriotic songs. In 1947, he became a poet-in-residence at Atlanta University, and in 1949 he was offered the position of poet-teacher at the University of Chicago. In Chicago, he began to publish a series of short stories based on the character of Jess B. Semple, a kind of black Everyman who reacts to racism with infinite patience, humor, and quiet determination. The Semple stories were probably the most widely read of Hughes's works during his lifetime. In 1951, he published *Montage of a Dream Deferred*, a third collection of poetry that used modernist techniques to paint portraits of everyday life in Harlem.

In 1953, Hughes was interrogated by the House Un-American Activities Committee about his radical political associations, and invitations for poetry readings and lectures dwindled. But Hughes was growing tired of politics. Lending his name to controversial causes had cost him a decent livelihood, which was hard enough for a poet to earn under any circumstances. When, in 1959, he put together a new anthology of his *Selected Poems*, he did not include many of his angrier attacks on social injustice. In the last decades of his life he tried to produce several Broadway musicals based on gospel music, but they were only modestly successful with the public. He helped to promote the works of younger black writers such as James Baldwin, Gwendolyn Brooks, Alice Walker, and Imamu Amiri Baraka.

In the early 1960s, Hughes traveled to Europe and Africa as a cultural spokesman for the John F. Kennedy and Lyndon B. Johnson administrations. By 1967, however, his health began to fail, and he died on May 22 in a New York City hospital. Langston Hughes's creation of a distinctive poetic voice for black Americans made him one of the most important figures in modern American literature.

RICHARD WRIGHT

Poet, playwright, political activist, and the first novelist to portray the harsh realities of black life in white America, Richard Nathaniel Wright was born on September 4, 1908, near Natchez, Mississippi. He was the son of sharecroppers who grew cotton on a small plot rented from a local landowner. Tenant farmers like the Wrights were often in debt to the landowners and lived as indentured servants on their farms, which perpetuated the plantation system long after the disappearance of legal slavery. To escape this fate, the Wrights moved to Memphis, Tennessee, when Richard was four years old, but his father could not find work in the city and abandoned the family in 1914.

Wright's early life was one of poverty, and he often did not have enough to eat. His mother's health was poor, and when she could not manage he was sent to an orphanage or to stay with his grandmother in Jackson, Mississippi. At the Smith-Robertson Public School in Jackson, Wright began to take an interest in literature. He published his first short story, "The Voodoo of Hell's Half Acre," in 1923 in the *Southern Register*, a local black weekly newspaper. But he was a rebellious student, rejecting his family's religious fundamentalism and defying teachers and counselors who urged him to accept his fate as a poor southern black boy. He wanted nothing less than to get out of the South and to get away from the oppressive weight of racism and segregation.

In 1925, Wright returned to Memphis. He worked at odd jobs, saving what money he could, dreaming of leaving the South. In the city's old bookshops he picked up used copies of magazines, including H. L. Mencken's *American Mercury*. Mencken was a sharp-witted satirist of American institutions who had attacked racial prejudice, and Wright was amazed that there were white men who felt this way. Mencken also talked about writers who were unknown to Wright—

Mark Twain, Joseph Conrad, Fyodor Dostoyevsky, and Leo Tolstoy—and Wright was fascinated. Blacks were not permitted to take books out of the local library, so Wright asked a young white friend for the use of his library card and began to read both the classics and the new American writers—Theodore Dreiser, Sherwood Anderson, Sinclair Lewis, and Mencken himself—who were savagely attacking social injustice and prejudice. Wright yearned to use words as weapons, as these writers were using them. Finally, in 1927, he saved enough money to leave the South, and the Wright family moved to Chicago, Illinois.

In Chicago, Wright got a job with the post office, but with the coming of the Great Depression in 1929 his hours of work were reduced, and he often had to stand on breadlines to get enough to eat. In 1931, he managed to publish a second short story, a murder mystery called "Superstition," in a local magazine, but this did little to improve his finances. Experiencing firsthand the plight of poor black and white workers during the depression, Wright's thinking became radicalized, and in 1932 he joined the Communist party and its special organization for left-wing writers and intellectuals, the John Reed Club. He began to publish protest poems in the party's literary magazines—*Left Front, New Masses, The Anvil,* and *International Literature*—expressing his belief that only socialism could eliminate racism from American society.

In 1935, Wright went to work for the Federal Writers' Project, a New Deal program designed to provide employment for writers. In 1936, one of his short stories, "Big Boy Leaves Home," was published in *The New Caravan* and favorably reviewed by the leading critics of the day. Struggling to develop his literary skills, Wright came into increasing conflict with the Communist party, which wanted him to produce formula works based on the party's views on black liberation. The party had dissolved the John Reed clubs because they were too intellectually independent, and though Wright retained his commitment to socialism, his relationship with the party grew increasingly strained. In 1937, at the age of 29, he decided to move to New York City, where he hoped to promote his writing career.

Wright moved into a furnished room in a Harlem hotel. Though he continued to annoy Communist party leaders by speaking in favor of creative freedom for writers, he was made editor of the party's new literary magazine, *New Challenge*. He also wrote articles for the *Daily Worker*. In New York, he met Ernest Hemingway, Lillian Hellman, and Archibald MacLeish, and he befriended two other aspiring black writers—Langston Hughes and Ralph Ellison. In 1938, his short story "Fire and Cloud" won a $500 Federal Writers' Project prize. In the same year, Harper & Brothers published *Uncle Tom's Children*, a collection of Wright's stories about the effects of racism on Mississippi blacks. The book was well received and brought Wright national attention.

By 1939, Wright was living in Brooklyn, New York, and had stopped writing for Communist publications to concentrate on the novel that would make him famous, *Native Son*. Published in 1940, it told the harrowing story of Bigger Thomas, an angry black youth trapped in an urban ghetto who is driven to commit murder and is sentenced to die in the electric chair as a result. Few novels had ever portrayed the pain of ghetto life with such uncompromising honesty, and *Native Son* was a stunning success. In 1941, Wright collaborated with Paul Green on a stage version of the novel, which was produced on Broadway by John Houseman and Orson Welles of the Mercury Theater group, with Canada Lee in the role of Bigger Thomas. Later that same year, Wright published *Twelve Million Black Voices: A Folk History of the Negro in the United States*, a photo-essay on black life from the Civil War to the present.

In 1942, Wright ended his association with the Communist party, which had continually hounded him to alter his writings and speeches to suit party doctrine. Ironically, as Wright's relationship with the party was ending, J. Edgar Hoover of the Federal Bureau of Investigation (FBI) and members of the House Un-American Activities Committee were beginning to investigate him as a political subversive, and these investigations would plague him for the rest of his life. In 1945, Wright published *Black Boy: A Record of Childhood and Youth*, an account of his early years in the South. Within three months, the book sold a half million copies. But in spite of his large readership, Wright was growing increasingly disillusioned. He was harassed by critics on the left and the right and placed under continual surveillance by government agencies. Praised as a courageous spokesman for black Americans, he still could not sit next to whites on a bus or a train or in a restaurant. In 1947, he left the United States to live in voluntary exile in Paris, France.

Wright thrived in Paris, meeting writers such as Jean-Paul Sartre, Albert Camus, and André Gide. The Parisians seemed free of racial prejudice and treated Wright with the same respect they showed their own intellectuals. He became involved in the Pan-African movement that sought to promote African culture and fight colonialism. In 1953, he published his second novel, *The Outsider*. Another portrait of black life in America, *The Outsider* was introspective and philosophical in tone, like Ralph Ellison's recently published *Invisible Man*. It was not as well received as his earlier works, and some critics suggested that he had been living outside the United States for too long to write about black life there.

In 1954, Wright published *Black Power: A Record of Reactions in a Land of Pathos*, an account of his trip through West Africa, and *Savage Holiday*, his third novel. In 1956, there followed *The Color Curtain*, a report on his participation in the 1955 conference of Third World nations in Bandung, Indonesia, and *Pagan Spain*, a book about life under the Spanish dictator Francisco Franco. In 1957, Wright published *White Man, Listen!*, a collection of essays that called upon the industrialized world to offer economic assistance to the nations of Africa. In 1958, he published his fourth novel, *The Long Dream*, but again critics accused him of being out of touch, of writing about the South as if it were still the 1920s and there was not a growing civil rights movement fighting to change things.

In his last years, Wright continued to produce short stories and plays, and he helped to promote the works of younger black writers such as James Baldwin and Imamu Amiri Baraka. He experimented with new forms, writing a large number of poems in the style of Japanese haiku. In 1960, he contracted a very severe intestinal virus and died in Paris on November 28 at the age of 52. No black writer before Richard Wright had done as much to expose the effects of racism in American life and to prod the conscience of the nation.

❦ FURTHER READING ❦

James Baldwin

Baldwin, James. *Go Tell It on the Mountain.* New York: Dell, 1985.

————. *Notes of a Native Son.* New York: Beacon Press, 1984.

Rosset, Lisa. *James Baldwin.* New York: Chelsea House, 1989.

Charles Chesnutt

Chesnutt, Charles W. *The Conjure Woman.* Ann Arbor: University of Michigan Press, 1969.

————. *The Wife of His Youth and Other Stories of the Color Line.* Ann Arbor: University of Michigan Press, 1968.

Thompson, Cliff. *Charles Chesnutt.* New York: Chelsea House, 1992.

Paul Laurence Dunbar

Dunbar, Paul Laurence. *The Complete Poems of Paul Laurence Dunbar.* New York: Dodd, Mead, 1980.

————. *The Uncalled.* 1898. Reprint. New York: Irvington, n.d.

Gentry, Tony. *Paul Laurence Dunbar.* New York: Chelsea House, 1989.

Ralph Ellison

Bishop, Jack. *Ralph Ellison.* New York: Chelsea House, 1988.

Ellison, Ralph. *Invisible Man.* New York: Random House, 1952.

Alex Haley

Haley, Alex. *The Autobiography of Malcolm X.* New York: Grove Press, 1965.

————. *Roots: The Saga of an American Family.* New York: Doubleday, 1976.

Shirley, David. *Alex Haley.* New York: Chelsea House, 1994.

Chester Himes

Himes, Chester. *My Life of Absurdity.* New York: Doubleday, 1972.

————. *A Rage in Harlem.* London: Allison and Busby England, 1985.

Wilson, M. L. *Chester Himes.* New York: Chelsea House, 1988.

Langston Hughes

Huggins, Nathan. *Voices from the Harlem Renaissance.* New York: Oxford University Press, 1976.

Hughes, Langston. *Selected Poetry of Langston Hughes.* New York: Alfred A. Knopf, 1959.

Rummel, Jack. *Langston Hughes.* New York: Chelsea House, 1988.

Richard Wright

Urban, Joan. *Richard Wright.* New York: Chelsea House, 1989.

Wright, Richard. *Black Boy.* 1945. Reprint. New York: Harper & Row, 1969.

————. *Native Son.* 1940. Reprint. New York: Harper & Row, 1969.

❧ INDEX ❧

PICTURE CREDITS

RICHARD RENNERT has edited the nearly 100 volumes in Chelsea House's award-winning BLACK AMERICANS OF ACHIEVEMENT series, which tells the stories of black men and women who have helped shape the course of modern history. He is also the author of several sports biographies, including *Henry Aaron*, *Jesse Owens*, and *Jackie Robinson*. He is a graduate of Haverford College in Haverford, Pennsylvania.